This igloo book belongs to:

....

Contents

Published in 2020
First published in the UK by Igloo Books Ltd
An imprint of Igloo Books Ltd
Cottage Farm, NN6 0BJ, UK
Owned by Bonnier Books
Sveavagen 56, Stockholm, Sweden
www.igloobooks.com

Illustrated by Gina Maldonado. Additional colour by Diane Kolar and Sophie Hanton
Written by Melanie Joyce

Cover designed by Vici Watson
Interiors designed by Kerri-Ann Hulme
Edited by Stephanie Moss

1020 002
2 4 6 8 10 9 7 5 3
ISBN 978-1-80022-489-6

Printed and manufactured in China

Stories for 1 Year Olds

# Bunny Fun

I bounce.

YOU...

bounce.

We...

bounce.

n c e.

11

Everyone bounces.

All **bouncing** bunnies together!

Tickle Time

Mummy tickles...

tummy.

15

Daddy...

... tickles...

... toes.

Archie **tickles** ears.

Elsa...

... tickles nose.

19

I tickle puppy.

kitty...

... tickles me.

We're a very...

22

... **tickly** family!

23

Here's the sun.

Here's a...

... bud.

Thud,

thud,

thud.

Water trickles down below.

Then the wind begins to BLOW.

29

Little bud...

... opens wide.

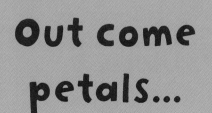

Out come petals...

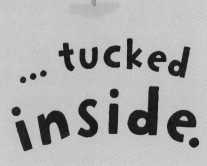

... tucked inside.

Look, it's the SUN!

Here comes a...

...shower.

33

Now Little Bud is a...

... flower!

34

Baby Burps

Here's your bowl...

... open **wide!**

Pop the **Sticky** spoon inside.

Soft and **Squidgy,** yum, yum,

yum.

38

Lots of
food...

... inside
your tum.

Drink it from your little cup.

All full now, one last...

slurp!

Pat your back and then a...

...BURP!

A little rest after your tea.

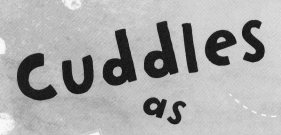

Cuddles as you...

...**Smile** at me.

Rock you **Slowly**...

... here we go.

Not too **fast...**

...and not too Slow.

You're so tired. Time for bed.
Settle down, my sleepyhead.